HOW TO READ THI

Are you sick of normal books always t[...]... the story's going to go?

I mean, when you get down to it, normal books really do have serious CONTROL ISSUES! You want the story of a book to go one way... but does it? **NO!**

Books always make their stories go exactly the way the BOOKS wants them to, as if THEY were the ones that were in charge. The nerve!

Sometimes books don't even seem to know or care what we, the readers, want! I mean, COME ON! Who do books think we are? We can't just let them push us around like that! It can drive someone CRAZY!!!

Well, if you share this kind of anger at normal books, then here's some **GOOD NEWS:** The book you're holding in your hand is NOT a normal book. It's one of those rare books that isn't selfish—isn't just thinking about what IT wants. Instead, at the end of each section it will ask you want YOU want.

That's right—Do **NOT** read this book cover-to-cover, as you would most books.

Instead, start at the first section... But when you get to the end of the section the book will give you options, asking you what YOU would like to have happen next, and then give you simple instructions on where to go in the book to follow your choice.

Naturally, as in life, you won't always make the right choices while reading this book. But don't worry... Unlike life, the book will always let you go back and start again, making new choices along the way.

The other problem with normal books—they never change! That's right, with most books, if you read them a second time EXACTLY THE SAME STUFF HAPPENS! How boring! How predictable!

However, the book you are holding right now will change as you make different decisions, and there are a few different endings you might encounter.

So rejoice... because now YOU are in charge of the story!

Use this power wisely...

● ○ ○

GOOD 🐝 LUCK!

THE BRAVEST WARRIORS ARE COUNTING ON YOU!

The **BRAVEST WARRIORS** are a group of teenage heroes living in the year 3085. Their mission is to help creatures both big and small, wherever they live in the vast universe. Why? Because everybody deserves a little bit of justice!

CHRIS KIRKMAN
Chris is the 16-year-old leader of the Warriors. He's brave and adventurous, but doesn't always know how to act around his teammate Beth, who he has a crush on.

BETH TEZUKA
Although good-natured, cute and fun, Beth is able to be tough enough to go toe-to-toe with anything the galaxy throws at her.

DANNY VASQUEZ
Sarcastic, mischievous, and free-spirited, Danny will always help you… Unless you cross him. Then… oh, yeah… You should watch your back.

WALLOW
Tall and strong, but loving and kind, Wallow makes friends with creatures from all over the galaxy.

CATBUG

Catbug is a Catbug. His favorite vegetable is sugar peas. His opinion on stuff is: "Stuff is GREAT!" Everybody loves Catbug.

...UM

...hember of the alien species known ...he "merewifs," Plum is mysterious, ...ring and somewhat cynical. She's ...e of Beth's best friends.

PRESIDENT MEMORY DON...

The leader of the Great Memory Do... empire, the President's natural abilit... allow her to control the minds of les... beings. And basically everyone is a lesser being.

...ROFESSOR BRAIN DOG 7

...at if your dog had a lot more brains, ...s an alien, and was a professor of a ...riety of subjects at major universities? ...that's basically this guy.

SPACE CHICKEN

A space chicken!

**That's all you really n...
to know to GET STAR...

CARTOON HANGOVER

BRAVEST WARRIORS

CREATED by PENDLETON WARD

THE GREAT CORE CAPER

[A THIS WAY OR THAT BOOK]

By
CHRIS "DOC" WYATT

Illustrations By
CORIN HOWELL

PERFECT SQUARE

Bravest Warriors
THE GREAT CORE CAPER

Author » Chris "Doc" Wyatt
Illustrator » Corin Howell
Book Design » Fawn Lau
Editor » Joel Enos

Special thanks to Jesse DeStasio,
Eric Homan, Nate Olson, Chris Troise
and the team at Frederator.

Printed in U.S.A.

Published by VIZ Media, LLC
P.O. Box 77010
San Francisco, CA 94107

Perfect Square Edition

10 9 8 7 6 5 4 3 2 1
First printing, October 2014

THE GREAT CORE CAPER

"Of course we'll help you," said Danny, holding his nose to block the terrible stench. "Helping little weird things is what the Bravest Warriors are all about!"

"Agreed," agreed Chris, trying to politely pretend like he couldn't smell anything. "Tell us what you need us to do so we can get down to biz... the biz of justice!"

"Thank you, Warriors," cried the Boss Goober-oid of the planet Goober-Delta-9. He and all the other goobers released their "body odor of thanks."

Instead of hand gestures or head nods, the Goober-oids' only nonverbal form of communication was bad smells. There was the "odor of warm greeting," the "odor of sad parting" and the "odor of frustration over traffic delays," just to name a few. The Goober-oids worked in gut-churning wafts the way great sculptors worked in marble. As a result, Goober-Delta-9 was always winning foulest-smelling planet awards.

The Bravest Warriors had been called to this uber-gross world by the Boss Goober-oid to solve a problem that seemed easy. But now that they were on Goober-Delta-9, they were realizing it might be a more complicated job…

"It's our planet's core," said Boss Goober-oid, releasing a smell of "fear for the future."

Turns out the planetary core of Goober-Delta-9 had been stolen! Without it, the planet would soon lose its rotation, its orbit would decay, and it would drift off into space! The Goober-oids would be DOOMED!

Worse of all, the core was being held in the most secure vault in the galaxy, beneath SYD BEEMER-BOOF'S Fun Planet™, the biggest amusement park planet in the known universe.

"Of course," said Wallow, a clothespin pinching his nose. "Syd Beemer-Boof is famous for his private collection of planetary cores. Only he would be ruthless enough to steal an inhabited planet's core, condemning to death a whole world of cute, gross freaks!"

Beth looked at her friends. "Warriors, this calls for a HEIST! That means we're going to need some help!"

As quickly as possible the Warriors assembled a crack team made up of beings with special skills, including...

Plum: an alluring Merewif;

Catbug: a loyal friend;

President Memory Donk: a master of mental manipulation;

Professor Brain Dog 7: a certified genius;

...and a space chicken: a chicken that looks like pigeon but comes from space!

Each one of these individuals had special skills that the Bravest Warriors were going to need to call upon if they were going to pull off this heist! The only problem was this: the team would seem too suspicious traveling all together. So Beth, Chris, Danny, Wallow and Catbug planned to go down to the planet, leaving the rest of the team on the ship.

"We'll teleport each of you guys in when it's time for you to use your skills, and then teleport back out when your part of the job is done," Beth explained to everyone.

"Until then, feel free to check out my collection of vintage sports cards," offered Wallow in a moment of generosity.

Everyone was happy to help the Bravest Warriors, so they kept busy on the ship while the Warriors and Catbug went down to the planet.

SYD BEEMER-BOOF'S Fun Planet™ turned out to be a truly magical place. The Bravest Warriors walked around wide-eyed and amazed by the large variety of rides, carnival games and freak-watching opportunities. Plus, nearly every conceivable food in the universe was offered either deep-fried, dipped in chocolate or both.

"Wow," said Catbug, when they arrived at SYD BEEMER-BOOF'S Fun Planet™. "I want to build a house out of funnel cakes!"

"Sorry, little guy," apologized Wallow. "As tasty as that house would be, we're here to do a job."

Finally, the team reached the first stage of their mission: BEEMER-BOOF'S KEEP™, the 500-story metal castle that served as the centerpiece of the entire amusement park planet. Around the back, guarded by a tough-looking security guard, was the door to Syd Beemer-Boof's private elevator. It was the only elevator that went all the way to the top of the castle...and the Bravest Warriors needed in.

That's why they teleported Plum down to join them.

"Okay, Plum," Danny said to the Merewif, "you're

up. Go distract that guard!"

"Distracting is what a Merewif does best," said Plum, heading off.

"Is that true?" Danny asked Beth as Plum approached the guard.

"Beats me," Beth replied, shrugging. "They're a very mysterious people... What do you think she'll do to distract him?"

If Plum fakes the guard out,
Turn to the NEXT PAGE.

If Plum offers the guard a
Space Lobster Dinner,
Go to PAGE 21.

TRUE LOVE

If Plum was going to pull this off, she was going to have to fake the guard out BIG TIME! She had an idea…

"You won't believe this!" shouted Plum, running up to the guard. "Some Alsmoosers are riding the CYCLO-MAT™!"

The guard instantly dropped his jaw in SHOCK!

You would have too, if you were in possession of the facts. You see, Alsmoosers were aliens that were only about a foot tall on average, but the CYCLO-MAT™ was a ride so INTENSE that you had to be at least six feet tall to ride it—as was clearly indicated on the

"You Must Be This Tall to Ride" sign at the back of the coaster's line.

And, while there were not that many laws on SYD BEEMER-BOOF'S Fun Planet™, the most important law of all was "never ride without meeting the height requirement."

"We have to stop this now!" shouted Plum. The guard seemed too stunned to move, so she reached out to grab his hand and pull him along...

And that's when it happened...

As soon as they touched, Plum and the guard felt an instant connection. Plum was so blown away that she completely forgot she was supposed to be keeping this guard busy so that her friends could carry off an intricately planned intergalactic heist. And he was so blown away that he completely forgot her claims of minimum height ride violations.

Recognizing what they had as the TRUE LOVE he'd been seeking his whole life, the guard radioed in for backup.

"Why do you need backup?" asked the dispatcher from the other end of the radio.

"Because," explained the guard, never taking his eyes off of Plum. "I quit! I'm getting married!"

As soon as his replacement arrived, the guard carried Plum to SYD BEEMER-BOOF'S COASTER OF HOLY MATRIMONY™, a unique roller coaster that started with a double loop twist and ended with the two riders in the car exchanging legally binding wedding vows. It was very romantic, but also had an intense drop that made almost everyone who rode it throw up, and some of them black out.

"Now the only thing that you'll be guarding...will be my heart," Plum said as the roller coaster pronounced them "man and mere-wife."

"I love you," screamed the guard as he threw up and passed out. It was all very romantic. Or at least as romantic as a wedding on an extreme roller coaster can ever get.

And so began the rest of their lives.

Plum and her guard spent their years together in mutual bliss on a remote part of the amusement park planet, living in a "tea cup" ride near a small village of merry-go-round maintenance technicians.

But, while Plum was happy, the Bravest Warriors were not. The replacement guard was not distractible, and the team never got access to that private elevator. Their mission failed. Without its planetary core, Goober-Delta-9 drifted away from its sun and eventually became unable to sustain life.

Being extinct, the Goober-oids never again won a worst-smelling planet award, though they were honored in the "in memorium" video at the next year's Galactic Odor Awards ceremony.

On the upside, however, Catbug hit the jackpot at the Fun Planet's Wack-a-Space-Chicken game, and earned ALL THE TICKETS EVER!

"I'm going to get my own private island," an excited Catbug proclaimed.

LOBSTER TROUBLE

Rather than get flirty, Plum actually decided that the best way to distract a guard is through his stomach. She quickly hit one of the Fun Planet's 7,981 all-you-can-eat buffets and used vast her undersea Merewif experience to select the most choice space lobster on offer.

"Hey, buddy," she said, as she approached the guard with the cosmic crustacean. "How would you like some surf and turf, minus the turf?"

As a distraction, it worked almost instantly. But not in the way Plum expected. The guard, it tuned out, had an exceptionally extreme, horribly violent allergy to space lobster... Something he probably should have mentioned on his intake paperwork when starting a job on a planet where space lobster buffets were the primary nutrition source.

The guard's rash was so itchy that he had to immediately rip off his uniform and run naked through the streets to the closest of the Fun Planet's 4,733 boutique spa locations in order to get a fancy skin treatment involving all-natural tree oils, petroleum jelly and embryonic stem cells.

Plum slipped into the guard's abandoned uniform as the Bravest Warriors and the rest of the heist team approached.

"That was amazing, Plum," said Beth. "How did you know he was going to be allergic?"

Plum shrugged. "I could just kind of tell, you know. He looked the type."

Seeming very official in her newly claimed

uniform, Plum let the team into the private elevator. It took nearly two hours for the elevator car to climb the 500 stories to the top floor of the castle, but it was a glass elevator and had amazing views.

"I can see our house from up here," shouted Catbug.

"Catbug, we don't live on this planet," Wallow reminded him.

"I can see someone's house from up here," shouted Catbug.

"Ding," said the elevator when it finally arrived at the top floor and opened directly into Mr. Beemer-Boof's personal office.

Beth rifled through the desk and the file cabinets until she found potentially valuable information in the form of draft contracts, rolls of blueprints and a secret diary that detailed Mr. Beemer-Boof's private hopes and dreams. "Is any of this stuff useful?" asked Beth, reading through everything. "Wait... Beemer-

Boof hopes to become an ice dancer?"

Chris consulted a set of blueprints. "According to these, we have to get through...there," he said, pointing to a high security door.

"This is where you come in, Catbug," said Wallow.

Catbug could periodically jump into an alternate dimension called the See-Through Zone, something he only recently learned how to control. The plan was for Catbug to travel to the See-Through Zone (where there probably wouldn't be a security door) then walk past where the door would have been. He could then jump back into our dimension and would be on the other side of the locked door. From inside, he could let the team in.

"Here it goes!" shouted Catbug over the staticky noise it always made when he jumped through the barrier between dimensions.

But as soon as he arrived in the See-Through Zone, Catbug noticed a bowl of his favorite vegetables,

looking fresh, cool and inviting. "Sugar peas, yum!" he shouted with glee.

If Catbug eats the sugar peas,
Go to the NEXT PAGE.

For Catbug to ignore
the deliciousness and focus on
his mission,
Go to PAGE 33.

SUGAR PEA POWER

"I deserve a quick break!" shouted Catbug as he ate all the sugar peas. Once they were all in his tummy, he moved on. Crossing to where he was supposed to be, he leapt back from the See-Through Zone into our usual dimension, and...

...Sure enough, it worked! He was on the other side of the security door. "Hey, guys, I'm totally in and everything," shouted Catbug through the door to the Bravest Warriors.

"Great work," replied Chris from the other side. "Now get it open."

Catbug moved to open the door, which had a wheel in the center that you had to spin in order to open the lock, like on a submarine bulkhead.

"Unnnnnghhh," said Catbug as he attempted to open the door. It was stuck! He tried again...and again, nothing.

"I'm just not strong enough," Catbug lamented. He was about to give up when the energy from the sugar peas that his body was digesting finally hit his system. With a sudden BURST of strength he yanked the wheel and opened the door.

"Hurrah for me!" shouted Catbug as the team made their way inside. Catbug realized that if he hadn't taken the time to enjoy a little break, he never would have been able to get the door open for the people who were depending on him.

Let that be a lesson to us all.

"Alright, we're in," said Danny.

As soon as they were inside, Wallow used a secure,

hardwired terminal to access the Fun Planet's security grid and shut down the motion sensors all around the vault. He also programmed all nearby security cameras to continuously replay a prerecorded loop.

"Now we can make our way to the actual vault," Wallow explained.

Once they got to the vault door, the team encountered their next obstacle: the CYBERNETIC SECURITY WEASELS that patrolled the vault door!

Beth turned to Plum, saying, "Thanks for your help with the guard, but it's President Memory Donk's turn!"

"No problem. Thanks, everybody, it was fun," said Plum as she was teleported back to the ship. In her place President Memory Donk teleported in.

"Oh, hello, everyone," said President Memory Donk as she shimmered into existence in front of them. According to the heist plan it was up to the President to replace the weasels' memories of needing to protect the

vault with some other memory. "Here I go," she said, as she got started.

To give the weasels memories of a pleasant weekend at the beach,
Go to PAGE 39.

To give the weasels horrible memories of having to spend time with their in-laws,
Go to PAGE 45.

CATBUG'S REGRET

Resisting temptation, Catbug pushed the bowl of sugar peas away from himself. "I need to be a strong hero and focus on my mission instead of eating all these sugar peas," declared Catbug. And he did just that.

Thanks to Catbug, the heist was a success, and the team got the stolen planetary core back to Goober-Delta-9. The Goober-oids were saved! Their civilization lived a long, prosperous (but smelly) existence.

Which was all well and good, except that...

Life took a dark turn for Catbug. Decades later, he still regretted the uneaten sugar peas. He obsessed over

them, painting images of them over and over again with finger paints, and writing long, depressing Gothic-style poems about them.

No matter how many sugar peas he ate, his sorrow was never vanquished, because no new sugar peas now were the same as those sugar peas then. He could have had them once...but he just didn't take the chance.

Living to bitter old age, the now elderly Catbug, leaning heavily on his cane, walked through a dark wood, only to be stopped by a white-haired wizard.

"You seem filled with regret," observed the wizard. "I'll do you a favor. Through my magic, I can grant you a second chance—one second chance only. You'll be able to travel back in time and fix a mistake you made in your youth."

Catbug thought about the offer. If the wizard was telling the truth, Catbug could finally eat those uneaten peas. But on the other hand, there was that other time, many years ago, when he was involved in a terrible war. Which mistake should he try to erase? The mistake that

had cast him into darkness or the mistake that brought war to an entire people?

"I will give you whichever second chance you decide to take," said the wizard. "But whatever you do, you'd better not ignore me, or you'll feel my wizardly wrath!"

If Catbug decides to go back to a time before he chose not to eat the peas,
Go to PAGE 21.

If Catbug decides to go back to a time before the Warriors fought a war in the army of the Clone Presidents,
Go to PAGE 61.

If Catbug chooses to ignore the wizard,
Go to PAGE 103.

VAULT SURPRISE

President Memory Donk's memory-washing worked! Lapsing into a nostalgic conversation about the time they all traveled to an exotic beach together, smiles jumped to the Cybernetic Weasels' faces.

"Remember how white the sand was?" one asked the others.

"And the shoreline stretched on for miles," said the second in a tone of awe.

"It took weeks for me to get the sand out of my circuits," laughed another.

Soon they wandered off, having totally forgotten that they were in charge of security for the vault.

"I wonder why we didn't take any pictures on the trip," one thought out loud as they walked away.

After they were gone, Beth walked up to the wall of the vault. There was no actual sign of a door. "So this is where the door is, but we can't see it because it has a temporal lock?"

"That's right," confirmed Wallow. "The door is constantly time traveling, always exactly two seconds ahead of us in the future. It will never manifest itself in the present unless a special 'time key' is present. And we don't have that key."

"Wonka-wonks!" swore Chris. "Then how are we going to open it?"

"That's where I come in, I believe," said Professor Brain Dog 7. The professor pulled a bunch of heavy, complex equipment out of a pocket universe that he always carried with him. Soon he'd set up a time-travel scanner array and started to time-hack the temporal lock.

"Eureka... I think we've got it, by Jove," said the professor as the door started to shimmer and manifest itself in the previously blank vault wall. But just as the door arrived, so did something else—

—a future version of the Bravest Warriors!

"Warriors, it's us, the Warriors!" said Future Danny. "We rode the time-wave from the vault door!"

Wearing rough, beaten-up clothes and looking like they'd been through many difficult situations, the Future Warriors wanted their present-day counterparts to come with them.

"In the future there's something important happening, and we need the help of our younger selves," shouted Future Danny.

"It's something that could affect the entire universe," added

Future Beth.

But at the same moment, the vault door opened. "I can't keep it open forever," warned Professor Brain Dog 7.

If the present-day Bravest Warriors go into the future with the Future Bravest Warriors,
Go to PAGE 51.

If the present-day Bravest Warriors go through the vault door and finish their mission,
Go to PAGE 57.

WHINY WEASLES

President Memory Donk exercised her memory abilities on the Cybernetic Security Weasels, planting hideous, gut-churning memories of having dinner with their in-laws.

"My job IS a real job!" howled one of the weasels.

"But I AM trying to be good enough for your daughter," whined another.

"Augggh... Your voice is so grating! I'm getting a headache!" shouted a third.

It looked like it was working, because the weasels

were putting their hands over their ears, slamming their heads into the wall and screaming while running in circles. They were clearly more than distracted enough for the team to get past them.

"Let's go," said Danny as he walked toward the door. Then he said, "Ouch! That hurts!" as one of the weasels, lashing out wildly and not knowing what it was really doing, accidentally bit Danny.

"You're being a baby," said Beth. "It's just a little weasel bite. It won't kill you."

But she was wrong.

The weasel had a particularly virulent strain of astro-rabies in its blood. The weasel was immune to this disease...but Danny wasn't. The pathogen spread like wild fire in his body, and he almost instantly started mutating into a hideous monster!

Biting and snarling, the Danny-Monster chomped down on Beth and Chris, and things just escalated from there, as they usually do when astro-rabies is involved.

Soon the whole team had turned into monsters, and the SYD BEEMER-BOOF Fun Planet ANIMAL CONTROL UNIT™ had to round them up...and put them down.

So see? Beth was completely wrong. He wasn't just being a baby, and it did kill him.

THE MORAL OF THE STORY: If you ever need to implant memories in a weasel as a form of distraction, always be nice and implant good memories. Kindness doesn't cost anything and can keep you from becoming a monster.

THE END

FUTURE SHOCK

"This man is handsome-looking, yo!" said Danny, looking at his future self. "In the future I become very rugged. War looks good on me."

"We have to go with them," Beth said, ignoring Danny. "They need our help."

"But can we trust them?" asked Wallow, giving Future Wallow a once-over. "I'm not sure if I like the look of that one."

"Ugh," said Future Wallow, rolling his eyes. "I used to be so lame."

"If we can't trust ourselves, who can we trust?" asked Chris. "Come on, let's just believe in ourselves."

Yes, the Bravest Warriors of the present decided to go with the Future Bravest Warriors, stepping into the time anomaly and WHIZZING through time to a war-torn, postapocalyptic future.

The Warriors found themselves on the surface of Earth's moon. They were on the rim of a crater, looking down into a corpse-strewn battlefield where two armies were locked in fierce conflict.

"Who's fighting who?" Chris asked the future Warriors.

"Get ready to hear this in your earholes, because it's totally WACK!" started Future Beth. And then she explained the situation…

It turns out that a fusion-cyborg being, made up of the cloned parts of various US presidents, was leading an army of time-displaced Huns on an assault against a Moon Castle, because inside the castle was a grain of sand that could restart the big bang.

"Clone President Taft-Hamilton-Lincoln wants the grain of sand so that he can remake the universe," explained Future Beth. "He wants to shape a universe way better than this one, with a lot more seaside vacation days, better parking and a much faster speed of light."

But the Moon Castle belonged to the Garbage Pirate, who was a pirate made out of pure garbage. Garbage Pirate held the grain of sand and was getting his army to fight the invaders in order to buy himself enough time to build a machine that could safely destroy the sand.

"He doesn't believe the universe should be remade by anyone and should stay the way it is, even if it has some flaws," explained Future Danny.

"Okay, so which side are we fighting for?" asked the Danny from the present.

"That's just the thing," said Future Wallow. "We

don't know what side to pick. We thought our younger selves might be able to help us decide."

"Yeah," said Future Beth, "on the one hand, more parking would be great, but on the other hand, there's something to the whole don't-destroy-the-universe-to-make-another-one-where-some-crazy-cyborg-clone-is-in-charge argument."

"Help us decide which side to fight for, please," the Future Warriors begged of the Warriors from the present.

To fight on the side of
Clone US Presidents-Amalgamation
Go to PAGE 61;

To fight on the side of the
Garbage Pirate
Go to PAGE 65;

To object to the war and
refuse to fight on either side
Go to PAGE 105.

TEMPORAL HEADACHES

"We can't afford to get distracted," said Beth, stepping toward the vault. "The Goober-oids are counting on us!"

The Bravest Warriors decided to ignore their future selves and go forward with their mission. The moment they made their decision, the future Warriors suddenly disappeared with a POP!

"What's up with that?" asked Beth.

"Probably, due to a temporal parasox, when you decided not to go into the future with your future selves, you actually changed what that future holds,

thus eliminating the timeline that they came from, so they ceased to exist," explained Professor Brain Dog 7, as he and the Space Chicken replaced President Memory Donk, teleporting in to play out their role in the heist.

"Ugh! Time travel gives me a headache," complained Danny.

They continued on. Inside the vault they found not one, but two planetary cores. If the team stole the wrong core and placed it back in the planet Goober-Delta-9, the planet could spontaneously combust!

"Okay, Space Chicken," said Wallow, setting the astro-fowl down. "Now's the time for you to do your thing!"

The Space Chicken was on the team because everybody knows that Space Chickens always roost on the most Gooberish planetary core. That's how the Bravest Warriors planned to discover which core they needed to steal.

But as the Space Chicken started to approach the

two cores, she suddenly was overcome by confusion.

Which one of these was the right one?

If the Space Chicken roosts
on the blue core,
Go to PAGE 71.

If the Space Chicken roosts
on the red core,
Go to PAGE 75.

WE HATE THE UNIVERSE

"Let's help change the universe!" shouted Chris.

"Yeah, it's not like this junky old place couldn't use some improvements," agreed Beth.

"I never much liked the universe anyway," remarked Danny.

"I'll do what Beth wants to do," said Chris.

So both sets of Bravest Warriors joined the armies of Clone President Taft-Hamilton-Lincoln, and their valiant efforts soon turned the tide of the battle. The Moon Castle was breached, the Garbage Pirate was put

in chains, and the grain of sand was used to create a new universe filled with seaside vacation spots, very ample parking and a really super-fast speed of light.

However, things went terribly. Everyone was spending so much time at the seaside that nothing got done...EVER. Economies collapsed, and all businesses were closed. There was plenty of parking, but once you'd parked there was nowhere worth going, and light was so fast that laser shows were hard to enjoy.

The whole universe fell apart, and everyone everywhere was miserable.

And it was all the Bravest Warriors' fault.

ON BEING GARBAGE PIRATES...

"Avast, ye landlubbers," hacked the Garbage Pirate. "So ye come to me side to fight on me crew, do ye?"

"Yes, the universe must be saved," confirmed Danny.

And so, the Bravest Warriors and the Future Bravest Warriors began what would end up being a very long battle to defend the Moon Castle against the attacking Huns. But as many, many, many years wore on, working with the Garbage Pirate became less and less cool. The Bravest Warriors may have agreed with Garbage Pirate about protecting the universe from

being radically altered, but they certainly didn't like him. In fact, the Garbage Pirate was actually a real jerk. He was mean all the time, and whenever someone upset him (which was, like, almost every day) he would make them walk the plank.

Admittedly, the plank wasn't as bad as it sounds because, since they were in a castle, after you jumped off the end of the plank, you would just land safely on the ground in the courtyard, and then you could easily walk right back into the castle if you wanted. But still, it was the principle of the thing.

The Garbage Pirate also was really into watching terrible TV shows. And everything in the castle (the food, the beds, etc...) was entirely made out of garbage, so conditions were deplorable. And it smelled. Like bad.

"This is miserable, but saving the universe is worth any price," said Wallow. But then he asked: "Right?" He looked to his future self for confirmation.

Not really knowing the answer, Future Wallow just shrugged and oiled up his bionic knees. "Philosophical q-q-questions are hard for me ever since b-b-bees ate that part of my b-b-brain," stuttered Future Wallow.

Hearing this, Wallow wrote down in his notebook: "Reminder: Avoid bees."

Danny played a lot of video games with Future Danny, but Future Danny always remembered what moves his younger self was going to pull, so Future Danny always won. Meanwhile, Chris mostly passed the long, empty hours by trying to bug Future Chris about his chances with Beth.

"Are we always just friends with her?" Chris would ask Future Chris, "or could it ever be more?" But Future Chris would mostly just get really quiet and stare up at the stars, a single tear coming to his eye. Future Chris was kind of a crier.

Beth, on the other hand, spent a lot of time in combat training with Future Beth, so as to ensure that she would one day grow up to be as tough as herself.

"This is how you kill a human with just one touch," said Future Beth as she used a test dummy to demonstrate bashing someone on the skull with a giant club. It was a brutal hit, but technically it was just one touch.

"Gee," thought Beth, "my future self is pretty hardcore..."

Everything became very routine...

One night a carrier pigeon flew in through the

window of the Bravest Warriors' bedroom (they all had to share the ONE room) with a note attached to it from the Clone President Taft-Hamilton-Lincoln.

"What's it say?" asked Chris.

Beth read the note to the other Warriors out loud:

"Four score and a while back, you came to fight for the Garbage Pirate. But I'll bet he's no fun to work with.

What a jerk! Come to me and switch sides. We'll make the universe a BETTER PLACE.

"Yours sincerely,

"Various Presidents."

"It's an offer worth thinking about," said Wallow.

"What should we do?" asked Chris.

If they change their minds and go fight for the Clone Presidents,
Go to PAGE 61.

To stick to your guns and fight for the Garbage Pirate,

Go to PAGE 93.

SPACE CHICKEN LOGIC

The Space Chicken was, like, totally confused... but she was trying to pull it together under pressure, since everyone was looking at her (a situation that would make anyone nervous, even a space chicken).

Finally, the Space Chicken went to roost on the blue planetary core.

It was the wrong decision.

It was a decision so wrong that it violently RIPPED a hole through all of space-time, and everyone on the team was sent backwards in time twenty-four hours.

You'd hope that the team would use this mistake to help them make better decisions the second time around. And hey, maybe they will, because they've got a whole day to think about it all over again, right?

Go BACK to PAGE 7.

SPACE CHICKEN'S CHOICE

Totally confused, but trying to pull it together under pressure (you know, since everyone was looking at it and making it nervous and everything) the Space Chicken almost made the wrong choice and sat on the blue core, which would have been a disaster, of course.

But at the last second, she took a moment to calm down, breathe, clear her chakras and trust her cosmic instincts.

The Space Chicken instead roosted on the red core.

It was the right choice!

"Hurrah, Space Chicken!" shouted Wallow.

"Nice work!" shouted Beth.

"Let's eat him!" shouted Catbug.

The team grabbed the core and raced back to their ship, charting a course for Goober-Delta-9.

"We're going to save them all," cheered Chris. They were almost close enough to beam the core back into the center of the planet and restore it to perfect working order.

But at that moment the whale ship's alarms went

off as one of SYD BEEMER-BOOF'S Fun Planet HEAVY WAR SPACE CRUISERS™ zipped into view.

Suddenly, an image of Mr. Syd Beemer-Boof himself appeared on-screen and called out to them.

"Bravest Warriors," shouted Beemer-Boof, "what you have stolen is the prize of my core collection. If you put that core back in that planet, I will destroy your ship with my SYD BEAMER-BOOF FUN MEGA-MISSLES™! But if you beam the core to me right now, I promise not to kill you. In fact, I will give you all jobs."

It was true, in their little ship the Bravest Warriors had little chance of withstanding an attack from a heavy war cruiser... But on the other hand, they'd gone through so much, could they really give up now and let this planet die?

If the Bravest Warriors
attack the war cruiser,
Go to THE NEXT PAGE.

If the Bravest Warriors
give Beemer-Boof the Core,
Go to PAGE 85.

If the Bravest Warriors
return the core to the planet,
Go to PAGE 97.

DUM WARRIORS

"Attack!" cried Danny.

Wallow turned the ship around, and Beth and Chris began to fire on the war cruiser!

Outgunned, outnumbered and outmatched, the Bravest Warriors fought anyway, willing to give everything they had in order to save a planet of weird, smelly little creatures!

They don't call them the BRAVEST Warriors for nothing!

They also don't call them the SMARTEST warriors.

Syd Beemer-Boof returned fire...

...and within seconds they weren't the Bravest Warriors...they were the Ghosts of the Bravest Warriors.

Whoops.

"I think I hate being dead," Ghost Danny said to the other Ghost Warriors.

"Let's see what we can do about that," suggested Ghost Wallow.

Soon the spirits of the dead Bravest Warriors had collected enough spirit matter to build a reality-warping device.

"Here goes nothing," said Ghost Beth as she threw the switch.

"Ka-chunk, ka-chunk," said the machine as it started WARPING the reality around them.

"We did it!" shouted Ghost Chris.

Suddenly, the Warriors found themselves alive

again, at a place they never expected to be!

"But where are we?" cried out Beth.

INSTRUCTIONS:
Flip through the book
and pick a random page…
Continue your adventure from there!

MR COTTON CANDY™

"There's no way we can beat him," said Chris.

"If we return the core to the planet, he'll just kill us and take the core again anyway," replied Danny glumly.

"Either way, the planet dies," Wallow sighed.

"Mr. Beemer-Boof, we give up," reported Beth to the view-screen. "We're beaming you the core now."

"We could have fought, but we didn't," said a saddened Wallow. "No longer are we the BRAVEST Warriors... From now on we shall be known as the Cowardliest Warriors."

Utterly defeated, and cursed by thoughts of the dying planet that they could not save, the Cowardliest Warriors were forced to work for Syd Beemer-Boof on SYD BEEMER-BOOF'S Fun Planet™ from then on.

Beth became a concession stand worker, Wallow a ride ticket-taker, Chris a costumed mascot named Mr. Cotton Candy and Danny a robot statue outside a spaceship ride.

For his work, Danny dressed as MARKY THE HAPPY SCREECH-OWL™. The costume had a giant fake head with a huge smile on it. No one could see that inside, Danny was frowning all day long for the rest of his life.

WHATEVER HAPPENED TO JELLY LAD

Impossibear rode the purple antelope around in circles, screaming, as the stone walls of the dungeon slowly closed in on them!

"There's no way out of here!" he shouted. "This is not the way Impossibear was supposed to die!"

"Quiet!" shouted Catbug, remaining cool and calm. "There's always a way!"

But despite his words, Catbug really did think that the situation was getting pretty bad.

Catbug looked over at Jelly Kid, who was cowering

in fear nearby.

"If this is the end anyway, should I just eat him?" thought Catbug, realizing how delicious Jelly Kid must be. "I mean it's not like he could create a set of stairs to get us out of here."

That's when he got the idea.

"Hey, Jelly Kid, make a bunch of bread and stuff," commanded Catbug, "and build us some stairs out of bread and stuff!"

Oh yeah! Why didn't they think of that before?

Jelly Kid, who had the ability to make bread appear out of thin air, started producing slice after slice, quickly building a soft, mushy, carbo-load of an escape stairway.

"My idea worked!" shouted Impossibear, as he rode the antelope up the bread stairs to freedom. "I saved the day!"

But Jelly Kid and Catbug shared a knowing look

as they climbed the stairs. They knew who had really saved the day.

They were free, and all was right with the world again!

Later, Catbug ate Jelly Kid.

He was delicious.

LOOPHOLE

The Bravest Warriors spent years fiercely defending the Moon Castle from the attacking Huns, by means of cattle-pults, skeleton bombs and anything else they could think of. Just as it seemed like their defenses were on their last legs, the Garbage Pirate's R&D team finally created the machine that would destroy the grain of sand.

"Here we go!" shouted the Garbage Pirate, putting the grain in the machine and pulling the lever, which was shaped like a rubber ducky for some reason.

Within moments, it was done. All power drained

from the sand, and it was useless. The universe was protected, and the Clone US Presidents-Amalgam would never again have reason to attack.

Suddenly, the Garbage Pirate was TRANSFORMED into a handsome young prince. "Ah, my old self again," he said, delighted! He'd had been trapped by the power of the sand, twisted into an unpleasant form. That was the reason he'd been so crabby, and that was the reason he'd watched all those bad TV shows!

"I'm sorry if living with me all these years was

difficult," he said to the Bravest Warriors. "Curse and all that, you know?"

"No problem," said Beth, who felt like maybe the curse didn't explain everything...because, let's be honest, a rich young prince of a Garbage Pirate is still a Garbage Pirate...

"Anytime you need the universe saved, you know who to call," shouted Wallow.

"Whatever, glad this is finally over," said Danny.

"Let's get out of here," said Chris.

The Future Bravest Warriors smiled at the Bravest Warriors. "You've done good work here, kids," said Future Beth.

No longer needed, the Future Bravest Warriors returned the regular Bravest Warriors back in time to the exact second from which they'd left.

"Oh, I thought you said you were going somewhere," said Professor Brain Dog 7.

"We did," Chris started to explain, before Beth interrupted him.

"That's right, we're in the middle of a mission. Come on, let's get back to what we were doing!"

Go to PAGE 57.

HIGH MOOP LEVELS

"Bravest Warriors ALWAYS help those in need, no matter the personal risk!" shouted Chris as he beamed the core back into the planet.

Restored, the planet instantly regained its proper gravity and rotation! The orbital decay was over! The Goober-oid people were SAVED!

"Hurray for the Bravest Warriors!" shouted millions of Goober-oids across the face of Goober-Delta-9 as they released their odors of extreme-happiness-and-hope-for-the-future!

But at that moment, above the planet, the war

cruiser was bearing down on the Bravest Warriors'
ship, firing all its weapons and bent on destruction.

"Um...yikes!" shouted Wallow as he did the
fanciest flying that he knew how to do! Barely evading
the fire, the Bravest Warriors stayed inches ahead of
destruction!

"What should we do now?" asked Chris.

"This situation is really raising my moop levels!"
yelled Danny.

That's when Beth realized that their only hope lay
in their half-insect, half-feline friend. "Catbug!" shouted
Beth, "how much control over your See-Through Zone
jumps do you have now?"

"I've been practicing and practicing!" Catbug stated proudly.

"Could you make the whole whale ship jump there?" Beth asked.

"I can sure try!" Catbug replied happily.

And—KA-BOOOOOOSH!!! He did it! The whole ship jumped briefly into the See-Through Zone right as the war cruiser's missiles passed through the space the ship had just been occupying! Beth's plan had worked—for now...

"I can't keep us here long," said Catbug, his energy draining.

"But if we go back, Beemer-Boof will just shoot us anyway!" Danny pointed out. "Ugh! My moop is on overload!"

"True..." said Beth, thinking. "Unless... Catbug, can you bring us back to the normal dimension INSIDE Beemer-Boof's ship?"

"Here goes!" shouted Catbug.

KA-BOOOOOOSH!!! As the whale ship appeared inside it, the war cruiser suddenly expanded and BURST at the seams! Quickly, before he died of exposure in empty space, the Bravest Warriors beamed Beemer-Boof onto their undamaged ship.

"No fair," shouted Beemer-Boof. "I didn't know you had a Catbug!"

"We don't have A Catbug," replied Beth, giving Catbug a big hug. "We have THE Catbug!"

"I love to cuddle!" shouted Catbug as Beth hugged him.

Beemer-Boof had been defeated, and he knew it. Entirely within the Bravest Warriors' power, the Fun Planet owner agreed to:

1) Say he was sorry.

2) Give the Bravest Warriors, their team, and the entire population of the planet Goober-Delta-9 free season passes to SYD BEEMER-BOOF'S Fun Planet™ (parking fees not included, some blackout days apply).

3) To never again steal the core of an inhabited planet.

The Bravest Warriors had saved not just the Goober-oids, but all lives on all the planets that Beemer-Boof would have destroyed if he hadn't been forced to abandon his evil ways.

THE END

CHRIS "DOC" WYATT

is a TV animation writer whose work can be seen on current and upcoming episodes of *Marvel's Ultimate Spider-Man*, *Marvel's Avengers Assemble* (both on DisneyXD), *Teenage Mutant Ninja Turtles* (on Nickelodeon), *Transformers: Rescue Bots* (on the Hub), and *The Octonauts* (on DisneyJr).

CORIN HOWELL

is an alumni of the Savannah College of Art and Design with a BFA in Sequential Art. She's recently worked on *Ben 10 Omniverse* (Halloween Special) and *Hello Kitty* (40th Anniversary) for Perfect Square. She also contributed to the recent *Bravest Warriors: The Search for Catbug* art book.